CAN'T WIN PRODUCTIONS PRESENTS:

Letters To Paul

Volume 2

By Keith Hachtel

Edited by Michael P. Vincent

Dear Paul,

   I'm thirty-seven, Paul. I'm nearly forty! What in the actual hell? Seriously, Paul, whatever happened to my 'live quick, die young' attitude that made me so damned irresistible in my youth? Jesus… in my youth. I sound like a grandma. Quick, find my cane.

   Ted called me while I was at the hospital. We only had a second to talk. He told me happy birthday, and then some inconsiderate person a few rooms down decided to go into a cardiac arrest. The nerve of some people, right? All joking aside, even after all this time it feels good helping bring a person back from the brink.

   Her name is Tamera. Tamera has been in and out of my hall for the past year. You would have liked her. She has one of the foulest mouths you have ever heard. Unless, of course, if her kids or grandkids are there. Then, she's the stereotypical sweet granny. It's hilarious!

   I don't think she has long for this world, Paul. I'll tell you what…. I'll keep her here as long as I can, but when she finally makes it your way, you help her get situated and comfortable. I'm sure it won't be an easy transition.

Ok, Paul, I'm calling it. It was a long day, and I'm too damn old for all this shit. Haha! I've been waiting all day to write that.

Love Lacie
(May 21, 2019)

Dear Paul,

    I need a vacation. Sorry it's been so long since I wrote. I worked three double shifts in a row. Do you remember when I told you that Stacy was pregnant? Well, she had some complications, and they took her off work until after the baby makes its debut. They said they would get us some help, but we all know how that turns out. The head of hospital staffing makes promises that, even if she could keep, she wouldn't. That's ok. It means more money for little ol' me. Not that I'll ever have time to spend it.

    Ok... A quick night's sleep and I'll do one more double, and then I'll take my couple of days off. That's as close to a vacation as I'm getting for a while. Might sneak an ice cream bar real quick. Don't tell Ted, though. I promised I would lay off the ice cream, if he layed off the diet soda crap. Being supportive sucks. I asked him exactly what his wife was sacrificing in support. He said she's dealing with his lack of caffeine and aspartame. I'll allow it, but I'm going to sneak a little every once in a while. Besides don't I deserve it?

Love,
Lacie
(June 3, 2019)

Dear Paul,

   My God, Paul.... Day four in the bag, and they actually come to me and ask me to work a shift on both of my days off! I'm tired as shit. Today was horrible, and we all know about my love for punishment. So, obviously, I said yes. Fuck Ted, I'm having two ice cream bars tonight. Let me just give you a short list of the days abuse...

   First, I was groped by no less than two old men. I'm sorry, but my ass is not a stress ball. Stop squeezing it!
Next, we had the privileged rich woman who thought she was in a day spa. I'm sorry, lady. I'm not here to give you a massage. You will have to learn to love the bed and pillows provided.

   I'll give you one more, Paul. Five minutes before I got off, a kid… not a patient, just some random kid... walked up to me and puked all over me. Apparently his mommy over fed him candy and junk food and I was the closest trash can in this little turd's mind.

Love, your sexy, vomit smelling nurse,
Lacie
(June 4, 2019)

Dear Paul,

    That little bastard threw up on me... again! He missed my clothes, but still got my shoes. This time, it was the beginning of my shift, and no matter how hard I scrubbed that smell followed me around all day.

    I know what you're thinking. Why didn't I switch to my spare pair? This was my spare pair. My other pair got trashed last week by Ted's dog. He chewed them up good. That'll teach me to be respectful to people's new carpet.

    I told Ted about the kid and the puke, and he laughed so hard I think he choked on his supper. Serves him right. I just hung up on his ass. All I'm going to say is... that if that kid even gets near me again, I'm going smack him with a stack of charts. Little shit... Why would anyone even want one of those monsters?

Love,
Lacie
(June 5, 2019)

Dear Paul,

    I want a baby! They are so damn cute! Stacy had a baby girl. She was a little early, but her little 6 pounds is still plenty to love! She's so cute and squishy! I can't wait to go back in tomorrow. I'm going in early to see her.

    I told Stacy that I wanted her, and she said after all that she wouldn't give her up for anything. I don't blame her.

Love,
Lacie
(June 29, 2019)

Dear Paul,

    Today was a little tough. Stacy turned in her notice. Really, she just quit. She was on leave anyways. It really sucks, though. I always seem to lose the people I like here.

    Also, to add to the crappy day, Miss Tamera took a turn for the worse. I heard the doctor tell a colleague that she will be lucky to make it through the night, let alone the week. I mean... I know that can change. She's tough. She may pull through, but she's old and not well. I hope I get to see her one last time, at least.

This is what makes this job hard.

Lacie
(July 2, 2019)

I can't today, Paul.

Lacie
(July 3, 2019)

Dear Paul,

I've seen so much since I've been here at the hospital. I've managed to deal with most everything. Life and death are around me all day. I've seen people, old and young, pass from so many things. I've seen seemingly healthy people die over things that were missed. I've seen Cancer, self-inflicted wounds, stabbings, gunshots and so many other things. Anytime a car crash victim comes in, I hold my breath and just trudge through. Sometimes they live....sometimes they die. Last night though… last night was hard.

Two teens were brought in to the ER a couple of days ago, a girl and a boy. The boy went through surgery and had apparent brain damage. The doctor said it was too soon to say, but he didn't think the boy would ever wake up. The girl, who had been driving, only had minor injuries. They kept her the first night, and then released her. She never left, though. When they finally put the boy in his room… Paul, they put him in your damn room. I mean, it's not your room. This is a different hall, but the room set up is exactly the same. I saw them push you… him, I'm sorry. I need to stop writing in ink… I saw them push him into his room and she stood at the door and watched as they hooked him up. She was in tears.

I almost lost it, right there on the floor! I had to run to the bathroom, and I just broke down. I couldn't help myself. All I could see was you. Damn it! I haven't had a breakdown like that in years. I called Ted when I left the hospital. He was standing outside my apartment waiting on me.

I couldn't even make it to the door before I broke down again. He just held me for the longest time, and then helped me in. All I could do was apologize to him for the next several hours. He just stayed with me and hugged me whenever I started to cry again.

I tried to write you last night, but I couldn't. I'm sorry. I called in today. I don't know if I can go back tomorrow. I just don't know.

Lacie
(July 4, 2019)

Dear Paul,

    Ted and Karen came over and spent most of the night with me. It's about one in the morning now. I think I'll be able to go in tomorrow, as long as I can get to sleep. They were a big help. I just needed time to deal with everything. I don't know why I took this one so personally. I've seen car wreck victims before. I guess that girl being so unwilling to leave the boys' side just hit me hard.

    Ted told me I was brave, and he has always been so proud of what I've become. It felt good. I've managed nearly thirteen years doing this, and this is my first real breakdown.

    I'll be honest with you, Paul. I bought a bottle of wine about two years ago, for a gift I never gave. It's been sitting on top of my fridge since I bought it. I haven't had a drink since that night. But I was so close to opening it. If Karen and Ted hadn't shown up, I'm not sure what I would have done, but that bottle would have been empty.

Lacie
(July 5, 2019)

Dear Paul,

   I made it through the day. I did all I could to avoid that room, but, eventually I had to face the inevitable.

   The boy's name is Jeremiah and the girl is Kate. They're from our town, Paul. They were out doing what all the kids in that shithole do… drinking and driving. I don't know why this happens so damn much. Our town apparently produces a lot of idiots. Drink at home. Drink in a field. Drink at a friend's house. Don't fucking drink and drive!

   She was driving and missed a curve. Now, her boyfriend is lying in that bed, barely alive. If he doesn't get better though, I can see that she might as well have died in that crash. Because she's not going to make it.

   Ted brought me lunch, and checked in on me. He said I was a little pale, but I seemed to be holding it together well. I promise you though, if someone would have even touched me, I probably would have hit the floor. I was such a wreck.

   I'm home now though, and I'm not sure that bottle will make the night. But, I'll try ice cream first. I hope it has double the chocolate on the stick.

Love,
Lacie

(Evening of July 5, 2019)

Dear Paul,

I can't lie. I opened the bottle last night. I sniffed it and almost threw up. I guess that little, hard core, girl you used to know only had one shot at Rock and Roll Heaven and she missed it. C'est la vie... I stuck with the ice cream. I just doubled up. You can tell Ted if you want to. I won't deny it.

I talked to the girl, Kate, today. It took me a few tries, but she finally started to show signs of life after my third round or so. She's related to some people who knew my mom and dad. I didn't really know more than a name.

She said they were out partying at a friend's house when her desire for tacos overtook her. This kid is messed up over damn tacos! Apparently, the boy didn't want her to go, but she gave him no other option. So, he rode with her since he was more drunk than she was.

She told me that she really liked him, but had planned to break up with him that night. But they were having fun and it never came up. The more I listened, the more I realized just how dumb kids are. Why the hell would we even allow them to date? She wanted to just break up with him, even though she really liked him. Dumb.

Were we really that dumb? I mean… yeah, ok. We really were that dumb. There's no question. Ted just called while I was writing. He and Karen are on their way over again. I keep telling him I don't like to answer calls. Text me, Ted. Jesus. Then his old ass calls. I think he fears the modern world. Anyways, I'll go for the night. I sure could use a kind word in my dreams tonight, Paul. I hope I see you.

Love,
Lacie
(July 6, 2019)

Dear Paul,

Oh, my God, Paul! Paul, oh my God! Ted and Karen just freaking left! They came to tell me that they're trying to have a baby!!! No shit! Why the hell would they even try?

They're old! Hell, Ted's so old, he's probably shooting blanks. I actually said that to him. I'm so excited for them, but I'm not babysitting.

Ok. Maybe once or twice when it's little.

Again,
Love,
Lacie
(July 6, 2019)

Dear Paul,

It's been a few days since I wrote you. They had me on doubles...again. That's not too bad, though. I've been talking with Kate. She's a fairly smart kid. She spends all day here, with Jeremiah and his mother. His mother doesn't blame her for the accident.

I'm really not sure I could have been that forgiving if it was my son, though. Maybe that's wrong of me. Especially after what I did. I mean, I know I wasn't driving, but I still feel like it's my fault you left in the first place.

I guess the boy's mother is a good person. Maybe I'm not. Either way, I've done what I can to help them. I guess I feel guilty for initially flipping out over their situation. Or, maybe it's still just about you, Paul. I mean, here I am, and all these years later, still writing you like you're coming home one day.

God I wish you were.

Lacie,
(July 12, 2019)

Dear Paul,

Ok.... I just need to breathe, but I'm not sure if I can. My patient died today. Miss Tamera left during my shift.

I'm not sure if I can get through this. I almost called Ted, but I don't need to keep bothering them. I just need to breath.

Lacie
(July 13, 2019)

Dear Paul,

    Yesterday was hard, Paul. I cried, right alongside Miss Tamera's daughter. It took me a while, but I managed to calm down last night.

    I just curled up with a picture of you and talked to you until I fell asleep. I'm sure you remember. You're always here with me.

    I think I'll go to her funeral. I don't normally do that, but I think I want to this time. I try not to bring work home, but lately it seems to be following me.

Love,
Lacie
(July 14th, 2019)

Dear Paul,

   The funeral was beautiful. There were pink flowers everywhere, and I found out some amazing things about Miss Tamera. She was a secretary for multiple generals in the army, for years. The things she's probably seen and heard.... Crazy.

   Her daughter spent so much time with me. I didn't understand that, though, because her family was there and there were so many of them. They would come up and say their apologies or condolences, and give their love. She would act gracious, but then turn back to me and talk about her mother and the life she lived. We even made plans to meet for lunch next week.

   Today was supposed to be safe, but I feel pretty good.

Love,
Lacie
(July 21, 2019)

Dear Paul,

    Today, Karen brought me a fruit salad. I graciously accepted it, but as soon as she left I offered it to Kate. I'm sorry. I just don't think fruit should be your whole meal, and a salad should be leafy and green. I did steal the mango though.

    It gave Kate and I time to talk. It turns out Kate is 2019's version of me. As Miss Tamera would say, she's a dirty little tart. She's barely eighteen, and already has several notches in her headboard. Jeremiah was her first real boyfriend. She said they had been going steady for maybe three or four months. Apparently he had been pining over her for some time, friends since childhood; she acted like she didn't know he liked her for a long time… Sound familiar?

    Thankfully, for him, she finally asked him out. She didn't get too detailed, but I think she was always in love with him. But she couldn't wait on him to make a move. Why couldn't I have done that?

    I thought seriously about telling her all about you, but I watched her as she waited at my work station while Jeremiah's mother had alone time with him. She never took her eyes off his room. One day, she might need our story, but today wasn't that day. She didn't need the idea planted that he might not make it.

Ok, Paul I'm going to bed. I'm off tomorrow. I think I'll go see Karen at work and take her some chocolate cake. Now that's a lunch. Try eating healthy now, Karen. Ha!

Love always,
Lacie
(July 23, 2019)

Dear Paul,

I couldn't sleep. I thought about it for the longest time. I used to be, for all intents and purposes, a slut. I got what I wanted. I never had any issues with who I was. I really liked who I was. Now, thinking about it, I haven't had sex in well over a year. I mean, what the hell?

I have to get my head out of this kids' world. Until my damn birthday I still felt like a kid. Now, I realize sex isn't important to me, and instead of a bottle of clear... I'm using extra strength acetaminophen to numb shit.

Lacie, again,
(July 23, 2019)

Dear Paul,

    Apparently, your death, and my breakdown and ultimate death, are legend in our small town. Did you know this was a thing? I know I didn't. I called Ted. He didn't know, either. Our names were lost somewhere along the line, but it was about us.

    I overheard one of Kate's 'friends', I use the term loosely. The little bitch was laughing! Telling Kate she'll go insane over her "little boyfriend's" death, and then kill herself. Who the fuck says that? What in the hell is wrong with kids these days? I had to tell that little bitch to leave. I hope she gets hit by a bus or something.

    I told Kate that that girl didn't know what she was talking about. She did her best to act like it didn't bother her, but it was obvious. She said the mean turd was just joking. She said the story was all about a girl from our town who killed her boyfriend in a wreck and then she went insane and killed herself over her broken heart. I told her the story was bullshit and the other girl didn't know what she was talking about.

    I mean, when did we become a cautionary tale? I'd be fine with it, if they got the right things to be cautious of… drinking and driving, leaving while upset, drinking yourself to death… forgiveness.

Our story shouldn't be reduced to a joke and a cliff note.

Love,
Lacie
(August 2, 2019)

Dear Paul,

    Paul Adams, do you know what the hell happened today? Do you? No shit.... I was contacted by our school, in our hometown, to take over as the school nurse! Then, no shit, they asked me if I wanted to join the committee involved in our twentieth class reunion and school/community events for the 2019/2020 school year. What in the actual fuck!?!?

    First of all, I would never leave my hospital. It's my home! Second, when the hell did it get to be twenty years? It was just yesterday… wasn't it?

    Apparently, they have a short list of alumni that became nurses. And since I had the longest experience, and a history of taking action (namely the petition to get you graduated), I was first choice. I can't say I wasn't flattered, but I'm not sure going back for anything more than a visit is a good idea. I can't say I would feel very at home anymore.

Your confused, and apparently old, girl,
Lacie
(August 5, 2019)

Dear Paul,

After the trash tale that was told to Kate the other day, I really thought maybe I should tell her about you. I even dug around in my boxes to find my old notebooks.

I thought maybe letting her read them might help. I don't know. Maybe that's not the best way to do it. Maybe I should actually talk to her.

I did find the first few notebooks, though it shocked me just how good my handwriting was in the first few. By the fourth, it looks like a second grader on crack. I'm glad I moved up to a fourth grade writing level… crack still notably in full use of course.

Anyways, maybe I'll see if I can talk to her tomorrow. It goes against my better nature to get involved, but I think I threw that out when I went to Miss Tamera's funeral.

Maybe this year has just gotten to me. Maybe it is time to look into another job. Maybe the school is something I should look into. Maybe.

Love,
Lacie
(August 6, 2019)

Dear Paul,

   Kate wasn't there today. It kind of made me nervous. I thought the worst. I had a whole speech planned out and I was prepared to answer questions. Then nothing.

   I overheard someone say she was having tests run on her for something, but I have no idea what. I might ask tomorrow if she is there.

   I did the only thing I could for her, though. I made extra trips to check on Jeremiah for her. I mean, it was the least I could do.

Love,
Lacie
(August 7, 2019)

Dear Paul,

Well, that was unexpected. It turns out, Kate is pregnant. She is in her eleventh week. Mind.... blown! I wanted to congratulate her, but I could see she wasn't really in the mindset or mood for that.

I walked into the room when she was alone with Jeremiah, and I saw her holding his hand against her stomach. She was crying and talking softly to him. I just stepped back out and gave her time. I'm not sure this would necessarily be a happy pregnancy.... even if Jeremiah wasn't lying in that bed.

Lacie
(August 8, 2019)

Dear Paul,

You know, Paul, I completely feel like everything in my life revolves around that hospital. The last three relationships, and that farce with the married (unbeknownst to me), anesthesiologist.... all came from the hospital. Other than Ted and Karen, I don't really have any friends. I have coworkers that invite me to baby showers, and weddings, and kids' birthday parties....

I haven't met a new person and just hung out in fucking years. Not to mention the fact, even though I just did, that I'm the only unmarried person working my hall.

Fuck my life, Paul. I have more in common with a pregnant seventeen year old slowly being overcome by depression, than anyone around me. Even Ted and Karen barely have anything in common with me, anymore.

Look at them, trying to have a kid. It's been a no-go, by the way, on the baby front. Now, all I've got is my day in and day out on the green ward, an ice cream bar, and some TV. Fuck, Paul. Just.... fuck.

Lacie,
Feeling shitty because I had the day off and thought way too damn much,
(August 9, 2019)

Dear Paul,

I had dream last night. I thought I would write it down real quick, before I go to work. It was a little bit disconcerting, but, at the same time I felt really calm.

I was old, Paul. Not like I am now, I mean I was really old... maybe eighty-something. I was sitting on a porch, next to an empty rocker, and I closed my eyes for a second then opened them and you were standing there. You held your hand out to me and I stood up. Only, when I did, I was a kid again. I mean, I was the same age as you.

You took my hand and we started to walk away, and I looked back. I saw an old man walk up to my older self and lean down to touch my hand. He started to cry. I stopped and looked back at him. He was so sad. I wanted to go to him, but you just held my hand, smiled, and shook your head. The only thing you said was "Not yet", and I turned to walk with you again. The calmness washed over me.

When I woke up, I spent a few minutes trying to decide how I felt about this. I tried to think about the old man and who he could be. I decided to write it down so I wouldn't forget. Maybe I'll think about it and figure out who he was. I wish he hadn't cried. Didn't he know it was my time?

Lacie

(Early morning, August 10, 2019)

Dear Paul,

    I decided to take my first Journal with me and have Kate read it. I think she'll benefit from it. She needs to know that everything may not go perfectly, but that doesn't mean that everything is over. Besides, she's got a baby to think about.

    Damn. There sure are a bunch of baby related things happening right now.

Wish me luck,
Lacie
(Pre-shift August 10, 2019)

Dear Paul,

Today, Jeremiah took a turn for the worse. He developed pneumonia. The staff is doing what they can to fight it, but it's not good. They made Kate stay in the waiting room, down the hall. She wasn't happy about that at all.

I was ready to give her my journal, until I came in and found out what was going on. I hope that, for her sake, this isn't leading to what I think it is. This girl doesn't need that. I know I lost you, Paul, and I wasn't ready, but I had more time with you… a lot more time.

On the other side of things, my 'personal life', Ted called and said that he was bringing pizza by tonight, and a movie. Apparently, Karen is out of town for the week. I'm not sure I trust his choice in movies, bit I'll indulge him for one night. The man has horrible taste.

Love,
Lacie
(Early evening August 10, 2019)

Dear Paul,

    Jeremiah is not doing well. Kate is not doing well. This is too much. I'm trying to hold it together, and you know what? I'm not doing well.

    Ted stayed on the couch last night. I broke down during the middle of his stupid movie. I didn't realize just how much it was getting to me last night. He said I had been looking paler each day. He said I've lost weight, and he and Karen could see it. I didn't. He was right, though. I've lost over ten pounds. That's not much, but he said it was noticeable.

    Today, at the hospital, they let Kate join Jeremiah's mother in the room. That girl never left last night. I tried to get a meal for her, but she said she wasn't hungry. I tried to tell her that the baby needed food, too. That only made her cry. Then Jeremiah's mom started to cry, and I held what I could in. My eyes were burning the rest of the damn day. I came home and started to write this letter.

    It's now three hours since I started it. I don't know, Paul. This may be too much. Maybe I should take some time off.

Lacie
(August 11, 2019)

P.S.
    I can't do it, Paul. I have to see this through.

Dear Paul,

    He didn't make it. We tried. The doctors tried. The infection was just too much for him. His mother was in the room. Kate had to be taken out. She just fell on the floor. There was no screaming, no crying.... she just shut down, and fell to the floor.

    I helped her up, and got her to a chair before they came with a wheelchair for her. I didn't have time to feel then, but I do now.
Is it wrong that I feel relieved?

Lacie
(August 13, 2019)

Dear Paul,

    I feel bad about what I said yesterday. I spent all day today replaying it in my mind. What really bothered me was how easy it was to get back into my work. I smiled today. How can I? As invested in these people's lives as I was, I smiled. I ate my entire lunch. I made jokes. These are things that someone who didn't just witness a death does. This is what I've done for years.

    I looked back at my journals, especially the ones right after you died. I didn't remember then, and I still don't remember now, screaming or crying when I found out. I was told I did. Or did they just say that? Did I fall down and just sit there? What happened next? I woke up in the hospital.

    Honestly, I barely remember that. I looked back at the journal to help me remember what I do of that. Is that wrong?

    Maybe I need to see a psychiatrist, I don't know. I'll call Ted and see what he thinks. He was there the first time. I mean, not that this is the same, or that there is really a second time. I just don't know if I should feel this relieved. What do you think, Paul? Am I messed up?

Lacie
(August 14, 2019)

Dear Paul,

   I looked up my old shrink online. Turns out, he's retired. Well, that sucks. I liked him. He made things better and always answered my questions. I tried to ask another doctor what he thought, but he just said I should come in. Why would I want to do that? I feel fine. I just wanted to make sure that feeling fine was ok.

   Ted and I talked on the phone last night. He said he thought it was fine that I was fine. I'm not sure that's fine, though. I told him that and said I wanted to talk to my doctor, and he said I should. Then, I was left with the whole retirement thing and phone thing. I'd ask you, but you would probably agree that I'm fine. That's fine.
We're all fine here, Paul.

Lacie (August 16, 2019)

P.S.
   It's just fine.

Dear Paul,

   It is not fine. It is so bad. Kate had a miscarriage, and then she tried to kill herself. I don't even know if she's alive. I've just heard things from Ted, who heard things from his family back home.

   They told Ted that her family came and took her home after everything, and she just lost the baby. Then she tried to commit suicide. I feel so guilty. I should have done something sooner. I should have talked to her.

   Sorry.... I had to take a few minutes. I couldn't breathe. I've taken the test of the day off. I called in a bit of a favor from a lady in admissions. She gave me Kate's address. She isn't supposed to, but that's our secret. I'm going back home, and I'm going to see her if I can. I need to talk to her.

I hope to God it's not too late.

Lacie
(August 18, 2019)

Dear Paul,

    I pulled up the road and saw a bunch of cars parked down the side of the road, in front of the house. I saw a few teenagers crying. I didn't have the guts to ask anything more. I just turned around in a neighbor's drive, and went to my parent's home. I was shocked they were there in the middle of the week.

    My mom sat me down, and held my hands, and I told her what had happened. She was so worried about me. I told her I was ok. I told her I knew this wasn't my fault, and that I just wanted to help, and I waited too long.

    Do you know what my dad did? He brought me a drink. My mom just about flipped out. He shushed her, and handed it to me. He said to me, "Lacie, this isn't to forget. This isn't to make it feel better. This is because sometimes you have to deal with pain and, ice cream isn't enough. Don't use it as a crutch. Just take a sip, stand up, dust yourself off, and know that life is never too much for you."

    I took a sip. It was the worst drink I've ever had, and I've drunk vodka straight from the bottle. I now know that my dad is terrible at making mixed drinks, and that I'm going to make it. I think you would be proud, Paul.

Love,

Lacie
(August 18, 2019)

Dear Paul,

   So, Ted and I were talking about everything, and I told him I still wanted to do something. He made a suggestion.... He told me I should take my journals, my letters to you, and I should publish them. I should make them a book. Is that dumb, Paul?

   Should I let everyone see our story? It was one thing to talk to Kate about it. She would have understood. She was going through what we… what I went through. I don't know. Ted said he would help me weed out the letters that would be best to publish. He said he'd help me every step of the way. I told him I would think about it.

   I took the week off, and I really think I might just take an impromptu vacation. I think the ocean is calling my name. Of course, I'll take you with me, Paul. I think we'll crank up the music in my car and just drive. What do you think? It will give me time to think. Might even buy a new bikini. Come on, Paul. I'm thinking a big, floppy hat, and a drink with an umbrella in it.

Love,
Lacie
(August 24, 2019)

Dear Paul,

It's been a month since I went on vacation. It's been two weeks since Ted and I started digging though my old letters. We've spent every evening going over it, and we decided in the end to send them to a professional editor.

Her name is April. She's going to go through, about; one hundred and fifty letters that we picked out, and whittle them down to a usable story. She's going to edit them for grammar, but not for content. The idea we had is to leave everything as is. That way, everyone will be able to see what my mindset was.

She said that she's free to start on the letters right away, since her last job was canceled. I'm really nervous. This woman is going to read my words and think I'm a crazy person. I mean, crazier than I think I already am. I guess I'll just sit back and wait, and let my work keep me occupied. Damn, I'm nervous, Paul.

Love,
Lacie
(September 21, 2019)

Dear Paul,

'Wow.' Wow was the word she used to describe my letters to you. I wasn't sure what kind of wow she meant, since it was in a text. I was too damn nervous to ask, but before I could, she called me. I was so hung up on the wow that I dropped my phone when it rang. But, once I picked it up, I got my answer.

"Wow!" She repeated herself, but, thankfully, it was an excited wow. She told me that the letters were short but powerful. Then she said something that made me feel funny all over again. "Do you trust me?" I mean, I don't even really know her. How can I trust her? So, of course, I said yes.

She told me to give her two days and she'll show me exactly what she has planned. Two days. That's like a billion years when you've put your heart and soul out there for someone to be "trusted" with.

Keep me strong, Paul.

Lacie
(September 23, 2019)

Dear Paul,

    Forty pages, Paul. She cut it down to forty pages and said that's all that was necessary. I sent a hundred and fifty pages and I have been contemplating sending more, and she said that's all that was necessary.

    What in the actual fuck, Paul? How should I respond? No! It's meant to be a full story to help people dealing with hard life events. How can forty pages be anything? Bullshit! She said she was going to email me a first draft.

Bullshit!

Lacie
(September 25, 2019)

Dear Paul,

    Forty pages, Paul. It was perfect. She managed to take the perfect set of letters and tell our whole story in forty pages. I cried, Paul. There was more emotion in those forty pages than I thought I even went through the whole time I was dealing with you in the coma and after.

    I don't know anyone that would spend money on a forty page book. Miss April thinks it will just sell itself. I'm not sure I believe that. I ended up giving her the go ahead, and she is formatting the book and editing my scribble scratch, and then she's going to set it up for self-publishing. And now, more waiting.

Love,
Lacie
(September 26, 2019)

Dear Paul,

   The book has been submitted for self-publishing. We made a simple cover that just has a picture of a letter and a pen on it with the words "Dear Paul". Simple, but nice.

   Ted and Karen are taking me out for dinner tonight. I told them it would be late since I had a shift at the hospital, but they said they found a restaurant with the best onion rings in Memphis. I won't lie. I could really go for some food onion rings.

   In other news, Miss Tamera's daughter contacted me at the hospital today. She said she lost her phone last week and wanted to make sure she had my number. We've had lunch three or four times now. She is just as amazing as her mother. The cursing isn't as prominent in her dialogue, but there is no doubt she is her mother's daughter.

   She said she wants to meet up next week for drinks. Apparently, her kids are out of town for a school thing. I'm looking forward to it. Anyways, I wanted to get this out before they come to get me. I figure I'll just want to crash when I get home.

Love always,
Lacie
(September 30, 2019)

Dear Paul,

Holy shit!!! Their old asses did it!!!! They're having a baby!!!!

Ok. Now, I'm going to bed. I'm tired as hell. Excited, but damn tired.

Lacie
(September 30, 2019)

P.S.
The onion rings were good!

Dear Paul,

    So, like I was saying last night, they're pregnant. I'm so excited! I'm going to be like an auntie!!! Auntie Lacie… Oh, dammit. Now I feel old again.

    They took me to this seafood place out near the Mall. They ordered, and got a large plate of onion rings to share, and then they broke the news. I'm telling you... it was so much fun screaming out over the crowd and the music that I was going to be an Aunt!

    I know I embarrassed them, but fuck that! I was excited! We even had cake and ice cream to celebrate. And guess what I get to do! I get to do the baby shower!!!

    Now, I was told to hold off on saying anything to anyone for a while. They're still early in the pregnancy and with their age it's best to see how things go. I agreed. So, like everything else, I am left waiting.

    That's ok though. I'm happy to wait. I love you, Paul. Wish you were here for this. It's going to be fun!

Love,
Lacie
(October 1, 2019)

Dear Paul,

The book goes live today, Paul. I ordered twenty copies to give to family and friends. Although, I can only think of like six people to give it to. Oh, man, Paul. I have no clue what I'm supposed to do next.

Should I just give it to random people? How do I promote this? Again, this is another time I wish you were here to help me. This isn't what I had planned to do with my life. I'm a former self-deprecating, alcoholic teenager, turned self-dependent, thirty-something nurse, not an author.

Love,
Lacie
(October 8, 2019)

Dear Paul,

I had my first sale today! How cool is that? Of course, it was my mom, but still.... I told her I had a copy for her and she told me to save it for someone else. Either way, I left her a copy on the coffee table. She can give it to someone if she wants.

I gave Ted his and a spare for Karen. Not that they didn't have a big part to play in all this. They've done as much work as I did, maybe more. You'll be pleased to know that the baby is coming along well.

They have Karen on light duty since this is her first pregnancy and she's as old as she is. They are taking no chances. Just think about it, this time next year we will have a little Ted toddling around. Crazy!

Love,
Lacie
(October 15, 2019)

Dear Paul,

    I waited to see your mom until today. I had a copy of the book in hand, and even though she knew we were working on it, and I never wanted to hurt her or your dad, but I know what I said in those damn letters to you. I wasn't exactly kind to them.

    Your mom hugged me so tight when she opened the door for me. I cried. We talked for hours, Paul. I apologized to her so many times she finally just told me to shut up. I think I needed it, too. We talked over what I wanted this book to do, and what I wanted it to represent. She understood.

    At least, she said she did. I hope she still does after she's done reading.
When I left, she said she loved me and that I was doing right by you, Paul. I looked at her and felt the sting of tears in my eyes all over again. I blurted out that I still love you and I write you almost every day.

    She hugged me again and told me I could let go. She said I deserved to be with someone who could love me back. I said you weren't here, but I know you still do love me. Then she cried. I didn't mean to make her cry, Paul. I'm sorry. We said our goodbyes after we both cried some more. I just hope she understands.

Lacie,
(October 21, 2019)

Dear Paul,

   I went to bed last night with a happy heart, and a perfect number of book sales, five. This morning, just for shits and giggles, I looked at my sales report page. I had seven hundred and fifty-five sales! I choked on my coffee. I couldn't catch my breath.

   By the time I was finally able to breath again, my eyes were watering, and I sat on the floor sucking in air. I probably looked ridiculous. I really could have died. Maybe.

   Anyways, after my logic button flipped back on, I realized it must be just a mistake. So, all day I've been flipping back to the report page and that seven fifty-five is still sitting there. Fuck it. If they want to pay me for their mistakes, then bring it on. I'm waiting on that check.

Love,
Lacie
(October 31, 2019)

Dear Paul,

   I was so hung-up on the stupid sales, no change by the way, that I forgot to tell you about my costume today. It was a replica of a nurse's uniform from the early 1900's. I had the little white, frilly, hat and the blue dress with the white apron and a nice red cross in the middle of it. It was really cool, although, it was a bit cumbersome to work in.

   I had to ok the outfit, but I had no issues. I did happen to scare one old man, though. He thought I was a ghost! We laughed so hard, after I took his blood pressure. He was just sitting there, staring at me. The look of relief on his face when I talked was hysterical.

Anyways, I would have P.S.ed this, but I thought this deserved a letter of it's own. Ok, I'm out for the night. I'm going to binge watch something and eat popcorn. Hell yeah, I'm a party animal.

Love again,
Lacie
(October 31, 2019)

Dear Paul,

It turns out; it was your mother who showed my book to the school board. They had a long discussion about the pros and cons of showing young kids something with so much 'graphic content' in it. Then, they voted to see if it would be handed out. Then they sent letters home to all the parents, discussing the book, and giving them a chance to read the content before they were handed out.

The letter basically told the parents that my book would probably be considered inappropriate in any other situation, but due to so many children being affected by the deaths of Jeremiah and Kate, especially with her committing suicide as she did, they found my spiral into alcoholism, near death, and my eventual bounce back, inspiring.

They felt that it could help, that I could help. I wasn't sure, though. Ted told me I should do it. He said that this was why we made this book public. He's right, of course. I wanted to help Kate and I waited too long. I really don't want that to happen again. I think I'm going to do it, as long as Ted is with me. I know you're with me, Paul. With the two of you, I can do anything.

Love,

Lacie
(November 5, 2019)

P.S.
   Damn it. Now I have to write a speech. Ted's ass is going to have to help me.

Dear Paul,

   Ted and I worked on my speech this weekend. I'm not sure how well it'll go. I asked the school what they wanted me to discuss. The lady I've been working with is Miss Chandler.

   She works for the board of education, and stated that she wanted to discuss loss, and how there are people around that can help when you're in a bad place. She definitely wants me to point out that I was able to move on, but I hate to tell her, I never really moved on. I'm still right here, writing you letters.

Do you know that, apparently, over ninety percent of the parents approved of it? Ninety percent! I wonder what the other ten percent will do. One good thing is that only Juniors and Seniors are attending. That allows for slightly more adult questioning. I know I thought I was an adult when I was sixteen. Yeah.

   Apparently, I'm supposed to answer questions afterwards. This is, possibly, getting a bit out of hand. It's definitely out of my league.

Love,
Scaredy Lacie (my new nickname), (November 11, 2019)

Dear Paul,

Ok. The date is set. Tuesday, December the third. I'll be talking with the classes of 2020 and 2021. I've been given the time as one o'clock, and I was told that the time is set for a quarter after for the actual speech and anytime up to two-thirty for questions.

I doubt they'll ask much. No one likes class participation.... Ok, I'm scared. I can't even think of anything else to say.

Lacie
(November 26, 2019)

Oh, shit! I looked at the calendar.... That's only a week away!!!

Dear Paul,

My heart is beating out of my chest... Ted is driving me to the school. I feel so sick... I had to bring you with me. Oh, God.

Lacie
(Pre-speech December 3, 2019)

Dear Paul,

It's over. I'm not dead, and I didn't have a heart attack. I'm still shaking, though. And I'm tired as hell, now. Give me a bit and I'll finish this. I just need a breather. Pretty sure I didn't breath all day.

Ok... I'm back. I had to let you know I survived. It was terrifying, but amazing. I finished talking and the principal stood up and asked if there were any questions. Paul, I think every hand in the auditorium went up. The first person I saw, in the front row, was the girl who came to see Kate in the hospital. I pointed at her and she stood up, and she said she was sorry.

She had no questions, Paul. She just wanted to say she was sorry. She stopped me on my way out, and told me that she hadn't realized that I was the girl in the story, and that she felt really guilty for making fun of Kate's situation. She hugged me and cried. I held her for the longest time. I never knew how hard it is for young people. They aren't ready this world, Paul. They're just babies...

I was asked so many questions. Some were about you and I, and some were about Kate and Jeremiah. Some were even about being a nurse. I got stuck on that girl's apology, though. It stayed with me.

I told you that I took you with me... One question that stuck out was when someone asked if everything I wrote was true. I said it was, and I pulled out the letter you wrote to me. I wanted to show them all that, no matter what, you were with me.

That's when I looked over at Ted and saw your mom was there, too. I swear to you, though, Paul... for a second, I thought I saw you standing there with Ted. And you were smiling.

So, all in all, I'm pretty sure I could go on about this, but I think maybe I'll let it all sink in first. Oh, and that time allotted thing? It went right out the window. They were still asking questions when the last bell rang.

Love always,
Lacie
(December 3, 2019)

Dear Paul....

That's how I started just about every letter. Some days, I wasn't quite as formal. Some days, I was so incredibly broken, that I held a pen in my hand and just cried. I think, in the end, the tears were more powerful than the words, but they weren't strong enough to save me. Not by themselves.

I was saved by the power of friendship and love. I had friends who were there for me, even when I didn't realize it. What you read were just my words. So many more people were dealing with the same thing, and some had it worse. I know that my best friend, Ted, was dealing with it silently. But even with his suffering, he managed to be there to save me.

It's because of him that I'm here to tell you the most important lesson you will ever learn... You are loved. And you are not alone. I know that some of you out there are popular, and you surround yourself with friends. That's the way I was. My friends Paul and Ted, though, were more selective. Many of you are more like they were, the type that has one true friend. And for that type of person, that's all you really want or need.

Paul and Ted were as close as brothers, and didn't really associate with many people, and even though I wasn't really like them, they accepted me into their hearts and I was considered a friend.

For those of you who think that you are alone, believe me when I tell you, I know exactly how it feels. I had points in my life where I felt that the world had completely abandoned me. Don't let the fear of solitude take over.

Look around... There are amazing people all around you, and I have a feeling that if you really look, you will find that at least one of them cares for you, and possibly so many more.
Another big part of why I'm here is alcohol. It's poison. It is a silent killer that took my friends life, and it took those of two of your classmates.

I know you may say that Kate wasn't killed by alcohol, but in the end, it was one mistake, one tragic night, and a few drinks that killed her. It took time for the effect to take hold, but in the end, drinking killed her.

It killed my Paul, and even though I was firmly against drinking and driving due to my belief that that man was the true cause, alcohol nearly took me, over a year later. I wasn't even in a car, let alone near one, but it almost got me.

I know I can't stop you from going out and being teenagers. I know that no grownup here has the ability to tell you that what you do is foolish. The truth is, the majority of us were just like you, and when we tell you what to do, and what not to do, it's not because we're trying to control your lives. It's because we were you, and we are trying to spare you the pain and suffering we went through.

I hope that, if you learn two things from my book... and from me standing here terrified, but honest... I hope you know that love and friendship can save your life, and alcohol doesn't make the pain go away. So, if you need help, if you need a friend, please ask. Don't be afraid. You live in an amazing time, when help is so easy to come by. You live in a time where being different is understood and accepted. And I think that with a little help, and lots of love, we can make the world a beautiful place.

Thank you.

*Lacie Henrickson
(December 3, 2019)*

Dear Paul,

Ted brought me lunch today at the hospital. He said no one should work on Christmas day. I told him I was happy to be there because it gave another nurse who has kids the day off. He said he understood that.

He also gave me a little present. I was tickled when I opened it. It was a quill and ink well. Get it, Paul? It's a feather, tickled? You need to work on your sense of humor, Paul...

It was still cool as hell. He said it was for the best writer around. I told him I would give it to her when I saw her. Humor, Paul. Find some.

However, I do have some news on the book front. Turns out that my little speech got around online. Some people caught it on their phone and it didn't exactly go viral, but it managed to reach out to other people who needed to hear what I had to say.

If it helps people, then I am happy and proud. Also, I was asked to speak at another school, somewhere in Mississippi. Ted told me to do it. I told him I'd think about it. Maybe this is my next big thing.

Ok, Paul, let me get some sleep. The hospital has been jumping lately. I expect I'll be asked to work a double tomorrow.

Love you always,
Lacie
(Christmas Day, 2019)

Dear Paul,

New Year's Eve, Paul! Tomorrow is 2020! I can't even believe this shit! You know what really pisses me off, though? No flying cars. Seriously, here we are, on the cusp of the second decade in a new millennium, and there are no damn flying cars.

Karen and Ted, and I, are going out tonight. Karen is the designated driver. Although, I told her she needs a bigger car. She's gotten a little bit chunkier. She said it's the baby, but I also pointed out that her "healthy eating habits" were tossed out the window. She hit me, Paul... The chunky woman hit me. It kind of hurt.

Seriously though, Paul, I'm excited! Tomorrow brings in a new year. I think 2020 is going to be the best! I have a couple of schools to speak at. Karen is going to make me Auntie Lacie, not to mention I am also a Godmother for the little beggar. I think that nothing can stop us in 2020!!!

Happy New Year!!!

Love always and forever,
Lacie
(December 31, 2019)

Made in the USA
Middletown, DE
14 February 2025

70876864R10039